Chapter One

Eight-year-old Sam was football-mad. His bedroom was covered in football pictures, he collected football stickers and read football stories every night. Sam lived with his Aunty Kathleen and Uncle Dennis in a block of flats in a big city. There was no garden, only a car park and a row of dustbins. So Sam would try and play football in the flat, with a rolled-up sock for a ball. But after he broke Aunty Kathleen's china lamp he was forbidden to play indoors again.

Sam asked if he could play football in the nearby park. His aunt said yes, if Bill Bateman went with him. Bill was an old friend who lived on the ground floor of their block. Sam rushed downstairs to ask him.

"Yes, I'll come with you!" said Bill. "I love football! I'll be your coach!"

The two of them spent several afternoons at the park. And Bill lent him his real leather football. Bill was a real football expert. He would do the throwing and Sam would be goalie, saving goal after goal. Sam loved to pretend that he could hear the roar of the crowd!

NO FOOTBALL

FOR SAM

by

THELMA LAMBERT

Illustrated by the author

3

HAMISH HAMILTON

LONDON

HAMISH HAMILTON LTD

Published by the Penguin Group
27 Wrights Lane, London W8 5TZ, England
Viking Penguin Inc., 375 Hudson Street, New York, New York 10014, USA
Penguin Books Australia Ltd, Ringwood, Victoria, Australia
Penguin Books (Canada) Ltd, 2801 John Street, Markham, Ontario, Canada L3R 1B4
Penguin Books (NZ) Ltd, 182-190 Wairau Road, Auckland 10, New Zealand

Penguin Books Ltd, Registered Offices: Harmondsworth, Middlesex, England

First published in Great Britain by Hamish Hamilton Ltd 1991

Copyright © 1991 by Thelma Lambert
Illustrations copyright © 1991 by Thelma Lambert

A CIP catalogue record for this book is available from the British Library

ISBN 0-241-12928-1

Typeset by Rowland Phototypesetting (London) Ltd
Reproduced, printed and bound by
BPCC Hazell Books, Aylesbury, Bucks, Member of BPCC Ltd.

Sam would come home from the park covered in mud from top to toe, chattering all the way to Bill about his favourite football team, Arsenal.

"I wish I could play in a proper football team," sighed Sam. But at his school they only played football for fun. They never played in a proper team against another proper team.

Every Friday evening Sam went to
the Cubs at St Mary's church hall.
They often played games – cricket,
rounders and football. One Friday the
cub leader, Akela, had some exciting
news for them. They were going to set
up a Football League with some other
Cub packs. There was going to be
a big Football Competition. Sam's

eyes gleamed: was he going to play in a proper football match at last?

"Now hands up – which boys are willing to practise every Saturday morning? Only those who train regularly can be in the Cub football team," said Akela.

Excitedly Sam shot his hand up. Unfortunately it caught Akela smack on the ear.

"Ooops! Sorry!" said Sam.

Akela rubbed his ear. "I can see you're keen, Sam," he sighed.

After that Sam went every single Saturday to the park to practise with the Cubs. Bill Bateman liked to go to the practice sessions too. Sam introduced Bill to Akela. When Akela

learned that Bill had played centre-
forward for Plumpton Rovers, he
asked him to be the Cubs' coach.

For weeks the Cubs trained hard. Then came the big moment when Akela chose the best players for the team. He chose Sam to be goalie, as he was the biggest, strongest Cub in the pack. He ran home to tell his aunt and uncle the good news.

"I'll need goalie gloves and shin pads," said Sam, his eyes shining. "And white shorts and a green top!"

"Oh dear!" said Aunty Kathleen. "What a lot of things! I hope they aren't too expensive."

Bit by bit Aunty bought all the football kit. Proudly, Sam tried it all on. Uncle Dennis took his photo.

One day after football practice Sam came home even muddier than usual.

"Straight into a hot bath!" ordered Aunty Kathleen.

Sam turned on the taps and tipped some green liquid from a big bottle into the rushing water.

"SAM! That's *shampoo*, not bubble-bath!" cried his aunt.

"Ooops! Sorry!" said Sam. "But

Aunty Kath! Our first match is on Saturday. We've been drawn against Westbury Cubs. We're going to play at their ground out in the country. Do you think we'll win? Bill says we've got a really good chance."

"You've got a really good chance of a clip round the ear if you leave the bath tub like you did last time," said Uncle Dennis, putting his head round the door. "Full of mud it was!"

Chapter Two

The Cubs were bowling along the
motorway in a blue and silver bus. It
was the day of the match and they
were on their way to Westbury.
Everyone was very excited. They sang
songs and chattered at the top of their
voices. All except Sam, that is. He sat
huddled in a corner with a very white
face.

"Are you all right, Sam?" said Akela.

"I feel a bit sick," said Sam.

Akela produced a bag of boiled sweets. "These are good for travel sickness," he said. And Sam stuffed one in his mouth.

"You'll soon feel better now," smiled Akela. But a few minutes later he heard a muffled cry. To his horror he saw that Sam's mouth was bleeding!

"I've cut my tongue on the sweet," he croaked.

"We'll be stopping at a motorway café in a few minutes," sighed Akela. "We can all get out and stretch our legs."

Sure enough the blue and silver bus

soon pulled off the road and into a
huge car park next to a café called *The
Happy Hamburger*.

"Now Cubs, don't eat too much,"
warned Akela. "We don't want
anyone else feeling sick! And make
sure you're all back here in half an
hour. We don't want to be late for the
match."

Sam groaned. The last thing *he* wanted to do was eat! While the rest of the Cubs went into the café, Sam made a bee-line for the toilets. And when he came out he felt a bit better.

There were a lot of people milling about in the car park, enjoying the bright sunshine. Groups of tourists were getting off their coaches, families with dogs were walking about, there was even another pack of Cubs. Sam sat down on a bench and began to read his comic.

He was so engrossed in reading he forgot everything else. Suddenly Sam jumped up in a panic: where were the Cubs? HAD HE MISSED THE BUS? He didn't think he'd been sitting

there long. Then in the distance Sam
spotted the Cubs in their distinctive
green jerseys. He pushed his way
through the jostling crowds. He was
only just in time. Sam clambered on
just as the doors were shutting. He
sank down in the front seat with a
sigh of relief as the bus pulled away.

The Cubs were much quieter now.
No singing at all. Sam settled his head
against the back of the seat, and
pulling his cap over his nose, he fell
asleep . . .

When Sam woke up there was
beautiful countryside flashing past
the window. He saw black and white
cows, a man on a tractor, a field of
corn. He caught a glimpse of blue and

realised they must be near the sea.
Funny, thought Sam, I didn't think
Westbury was near the sea . . .

Just then a large lady dressed in
Cub leader uniform came up to him.

"Who are you? You're not in our
group," she said.

Sam stared at her. He'd never seen
a *lady* Akela before! He looked around
the bus. He didn't recognise any of

these Cubs! Then to his horror it
suddenly dawned on him: he must
have got on the WRONG BUS!

The lady Akela began asking Sam
lots of questions.

"*What* a silly boy!" she said after
Sam finished explaining what had
happened at the motorway café. "And
what's your name?"

Sam told her.

"Sam Davis, eh!" she chuckled. "I've heard all about *you!* Well, you'd better stay with us for now. I'll try and get a message to your Akela when we arrive. He'll be very, very worried."

"Are you going to the football match at Westbury?" asked Sam anxiously.

"Football match? Certainly *not!*" said the stout lady Akela. "*We* are going to the circus!"

Sam's heart sank to his boots. No football for Sam . . .?

Chapter Three

A little while later they arrived at a seaside town, where a circus had its big tent in a field. But Sam just wasn't in the mood for watching a circus: all he wanted to do was play in a proper football team in a proper match and save goal after goal . . .

The lady Akela came up to Sam. "I've spoken to your Akela. He saw you get on the wrong bus but it was too late to stop you," she said. "But he knows where you are now . . ." She showed Sam where to sit. The Cubs were in the front two rows by the ringside, waiting for the circus to start. Sam asked them why they weren't in the Football Competition.

"We don't play football," said a small ginger-haired Cub.

"Our Akela says it's a nasty rough game," said a short fat boy in glasses.

"What *do* you do at your Cubs, then?" demanded Sam.

"Basket-making," said the fat boy.

"And we collect wild flowers and press them," said the small ginger-haired Cub.

"Football's better," said Sam shortly.

Just then the lights dimmed and the band struck up a jolly tune. The circus was about to begin. A tall man in a top hat and a handle-bar moustache sprang into the ring, lit by a bright spotlight.

"WELCOME!" he cried into a crackling microphone. "Welcome to Scattolini's Circus!"

There were elephants who danced very slowly and horses who trotted very quickly and a seal who balanced a ball on the end of her nose. But Sam couldn't really enjoy the circus, good as it was; his heart just wasn't in it. He began to fidget.

Then it was time for the last item on the programme.

"Ladies and Gentlemen!

Scattolini's Circus is proud to present a very special act! The only one of its kind in the entire world! Please give a warm welcome to the Footballing Chimps and Clowns!"

A roar went up from the crowd as chimpanzees and clowns, dressed as footballers, came running and tumbling into the ring. Some were dressed in Arsenal red tops, the rest were in blue. Two little goals were set up.

The ringmaster spoke into the crackling microphone again.

"Unfortunately Big Danny, who usually plays goalie, is sick. So we are one short of an 'Arsenal' player. Is there any keen footballer in the audience who would like to try his

luck? Come along, Ladies and Gentlemen! The chance of a lifetime to play for 'Arsenal'!"

The ringmaster walked round, trying to persuade someone to join in the game. His eye fell on the two rows of Cubs as the glare of the spotlight lit them up.

"Aha!" he cried. "I see we have some Cubs here today! What about it!

Don't be afraid, the chimps are very tame, they won't hurt you!"

But no one dared.

Then Sam stood up. "I don't mind," he said boldly. And he stepped over the barrier and into the soft sawdust of the ring. The lady Akela looked a bit worried.

Everyone cheered, and the Cubs yelled encouragement.

"GOOD OLD SAM!" they cried at the tops of their voices.

A small soft ball was thrown into the middle, and they began to play 'football'. The ringmaster was the referee, but the chimps didn't obey the rules at all. They climbed on the goal posts and swung round and round. They leapt on the referee's shoulders and stole his top hat. They grabbed the ball and stuffed it up their jumpers. But at the same time some of them *did* try and get the ball into the goals! Sam leapt and dived,

saving goal after goal, and this time he really did hear the roar of the crowd! Even the stout lady Akela was clapping and cheering by the end.

When the game was over, Sam was flushed with excitement and victory: 'Arsenal' had won 11-2.

In the bus going home Sam was the hero of the hour. He had saved the honour of the Cubs! They threw their caps in the air, they yelled and stamped. They sang songs till they were hoarse.

It was with a sigh of relief that the lady Akela saw Sam to his home. A last wave and a cheer and the bus was gone.

Uncle Dennis, Aunty Kathleen and Bill were waiting for Sam with a hot supper on the table.

"Well, old chap, how was the football match?" said his uncle.

"11-2," said Sam, his mouth full of baked potato. "We WON! But you should have seen them, Uncle Den! They kept fouling! They didn't keep

to the rules . . . they swung on the goal posts and tackled the referee!"

"Sound like a bunch of monkeys!" chuckled his uncle.

"That's just what they were!" said Sam. "SOME of them!" And he told them the whole story. They laughed and laughed!

Then Bill produced a big carrier bag. And inside was the real leather football. "This is for you to keep, Sam," he said. "I've a feeling you may be playing in a proper football match one of these days!"

Sam just couldn't wait . . .